D0167473

HELPING THE POLONSKYS

KHALEEL MUHAMMAD

THE ISLAMIC FOUNDATION

To all the hardworking youngsters in school and college,
and those embarking upon new careers,
who often go unnoticed but never fail to make us proud!

*Published by*
THE ISLAMIC FOUNDATION
Markfield Conference Centre, Ratby Lane, Markfield
Leicestershire, LE67 9SY, United Kingdom
E-mail: publications@islamic-foundation.com
Website: www.islamic-foundation.com
Quran House, P.O. BOX 30611, Nairobi, Kenya
P.M.B. 3193, Kano, Nigeria

*Distributed by*
KUBE PUBLISHING LTD
Tel +44 (01530) 249230, Fax +44 (01530) 249656
E-mail: info@kubepublishing.com
Website: www.kubepublishing.com

*Author* Khaleel Muhammad
*Editors* Fatima D'Oyen and Yosef Smyth
*Illustrator* Hilal Nayzaki
*Typesetter* Nasir Cadir

*A Cataloguing-in-Publication Data record for this book is available
from the British Library*

ISBN 978-0-86037-454-1 *paperback*

Printed by Imak Ofset - Turkey

# Contents

# Mr Polonsky's problem

SOMETHING heavy crashed against the hospital walls beside Mr Polonsky. C-rash! The awful sound was followed by a scream and half a dozen nurses pleading, 'Calm down, Mrs Polonsky! Calm down!'

A frazzled Dr Duffin pushed the door open and ran out into the hallway, barely escaping an expensive-looking glass paperweight which zoomed past his head and shattered against the opposite wall. 'Mrs Polonsky, please! This is completely unacceptable behaviour!' he shrieked as he closed the door behind him.

Now in the hallway, Dr Duffin turned to face a short, elderly gentleman in his seventies with a badly fitted toupee and a cracked, weather-beaten face, who was leaning against a mahogany walking cane, his features set in a sarcastic smirk.

'See? See? I told you she wouldn't take the news well!' he said, rolling his eyes smugly.

'Mr Polonsky, you must talk to your wife!' said the doctor, straightening his lab coat and tie. 'These tests are routine and ...'

Suddenly the door burst open and the old man's wife, Mrs Polonsky, surged into the hallway. She stumbled out trying to escape the grasp of the nurses who were desperately trying to restrain her. The woman, in her late seventies, had frizzled black hair that was turning white at the temples. After escaping the pack of nurses, she hurtled towards her terrified husband.

'It's your fault! It's all your fault, Shimon!' she shouted. Without her dentures, Mrs Polonsky's gums, with their remaining canine teeth, looked like dull, slime-covered fangs.

Before he could react, she clamped her bony fingers around his throat.

'It's your fault I have to stay here for two weeks – your fault!' Her hands began to close tightly around his thin wrinkled neck. 'When I get home, you had better make sure that house is spotless, Shimon! SPOTLESS!'

Suddenly the nurses and Dr Duffin were standing over him, laughing hysterically. They began to grow taller and taller, their bodies becoming thinner and drawn-out. Their features became distorted. The medical team pointed long bony fingers in Mr Polonksy's face as they screamed, 'Make sure that house is spotless, Shimon! Make sure that house is spotless! Make sure that house is spotless, Shimon! Make sure that house is spotless!'

Mr Polonsky awoke with a start. This was the worst nightmare yet! In the dim light of his bedroom he mopped his perspiring brow with the back of his hand, and glanced at the clock. It was 4am.

*Ah, Alexandra,* he thought to himself, *what am I going to do? You leave the clinic in a few days, but the state of the house? Ach!* he sighed heavily and moved towards the door. Walking to the balcony overlooking the lobby, Mr Polonsky shuddered. The place was a total shambles!

Mrs Gates, their long-serving and long-suffering housemaid, had finally had enough of Mrs Polonsky's appalling temper. Since then, the house had fallen into near ruin. This was hardly surprising, since there were six bedrooms occupied mainly by 10 cats and 15 budgerigars, as well as a garden overrun by 2 Billy goats and – at last count – 8 long-haired rabbits, all of whom needed feeding and grooming. Word must have got out to the local animal kingdom, because 5 dogs of assorted types from various houses nearby frequently sneaked into the house to hang out there too.

And, of course, there was Helga.

With his bad knee joints and arthritic hands, it was all Shimon Polonsky could do just to feed

the animals. Alexandra would have a fit if she saw the state of the house. She would no doubt call him an '*alter kocker*' – a Yiddish word for an old man past his prime. To make things worse, her unfortunate reputation and appallingly bad temper were enough to ensure that no one was prepared to lend him a hand. Mr Polonsky had called in a professional cleaning company from another town, but when the cleaners came along to look over the place they were attacked by the horde of dogs and goats, and one man had the seat of his pants bitten off! Unsurprisingly, they never came back.

He had to find a solution, he had to ... or else. But who would be silly enough to help him?

'Aha!' he cried as an inspirational idea struck him. 'That's it!'

He shuffled back excitedly into his bedroom and sat down behind his ancient typewriter. He put in a sheet of paper and began to type.

Cheap cleaners wanted ...

*No, that wouldn't do. Try again.*

Cleaners wanted – urgent! Long hours and little pay but at least I'll not be nagged to death by my wife!

*No, no! No point in being that honest.*

Mr Polonsky put in a new sheet of paper and started again.

# URGENT!

Cleaners wanted! Great opportunity for extra pocket money.

Only responsible, tidy children with permission from parents need apply. Report at 261 North Row at 10 a.m. on Saturday, May 3rd for immediate start.

Mr Polonsky leaned back in his chair and rubbed his bald head in his hands. A smug grin lined his face. Surely this was the answer. If he placed an ad in Violet's corner shop right outside the local secondary school that evening, some 'goody goodies' would turn up the following day and all his problems would be over. *And if the brats make a mess of the job?* Mr Polonsky thought, *well, I'll just blame the whole thing on them! Perfect!* His grin turned into a chuckle as he went back to bed. For the first time in two weeks Mr Polonsky slept soundly until morning.

# Answering the call

A tall teenage girl with a pretty purple and blue hijab peered at the typewritten advert in the window the following morning.

### URGENT!

Cleaners wanted! Great opportunity for extra pocket money.

Only responsible, tidy children with permission from parents need apply. Report at 261 North Row at 10 a.m. on Saturday, May 3rd for immediate start.

She re-read it aloud, '261 North Row. 261 North Row?' 'Hmmm ...' The address sounded familiar but she couldn't quite place it. 'Where have I heard that before?' she wondered aloud.

Out of the blue, a small Pakistani boy of about 13 ran right into her from behind, almost knocking her off her feet.

'Hey!' she said, turning around. The boy had had the worst of the impact and was lying in a heap on the pavement. He wore a white shirt and jeans, and had long hair. His baseball cap was lying on the floor.

'Hey!' said the girl again. 'Why don't you watch where you're going?'

The boy rubbed his knees and began struggling to his feet.

'Oh, so sorry! I keep falling over my own feet these days,' he said in a high squeaky voice. 'My name's Imran. I'm really sorry if I hurt you at all. I'm late for an appointment!'

The girl rolled her eyes and smiled. 'No, I'm okay, I didn't feel anything actually. And my *jalabiya*, I mean my clothes, are fine. Just … just be careful, OK?' she picked up his baseball cap and plonked it back on to his head, lopsided.

'My name's Leila. *As-salamu 'alaykum*, nice to meet you, Imran.' she added brushing down her dark purple *jalabiya*.

Before Imran could reply a boy and a girl on bikes came whizzing towards them at breakneck speed. They were having a race.

'Get back here, snail-girl!' laughed the boy, who was in pursuit of the girl. He wore a pink t-shirt and white trousers.

'Eat my dust!' the girl shouted back, the loose ends of her stylish hijab trailing behind her like a bright green and white flag.

'Hey, you guys watch where you're going!' gasped Leila as they sped dangerously close by. The handlebar of the boy's bike caught on the strap of Leila's backpack. It was whisked from her grip, but she lunged after it and was pulled along. Instinctively, she gripped Imran's t-shirt and pulled him along too. The extra weight on the boy's bike made him veer right and plough his front wheel into the girl's back wheel just ahead of him. Out of control, the odd-looking group of kids skidded and dived, all together, into a huge hole that had been dug the day before by a nearby roadwork crew and that was now full of muddy water.

Ka-splosh!

A workman standing nearby stared at the wet and sloppy bunch and burst out laughing.

'Bwa-haha … John, me ole mucker!' he said nudging his friend, 'look at this dozy lot taking a mud bath, ha ha ha!' Both men held their sides, they were laughing so much.

ROAD
CLOSED

The kids sat in a heap in the shallow muddy water.

Leila turned to the others and huffed, 'And to think I was going for a *cleaning* job!'

The tall boy, Adam, who was racing the girl in the green hijab shook his head.

'You're kidding right? That's where me and ...' he gestured to the green hijab girl.

'Sumaya, I'm called Sumaya!' she said seething with frustration and wringing water from her clothes.

'Gulp ... yeah we're going to 261 North Row.'

'Wow,' shouted Imran, 'talk about your cosmic coincidences ... we're all going for the same job!'

\*\*\*

Later that morning, at 10am on the dot, Mr Polonsky heard the dull thud of an iron doorknocker drumming in his good left ear. *The ad! Someone has turned up!* the old man thought. He jumped out of bed and made his way to the front door, undid the lock, and opened it.

There on his doorstep, completely covered in dripping mud, was a group of four kids staring back at him. Each had a mudstained sheet of paper in his or her outstretched hand. Leila spoke first with a bright and cheerful voice, 'Morning, sir! We're here for the cleaning job! Here are our letters of permission from our parents. Where do we start?'

Mr Polonsky sneered at them and clicked his tongue. 'So what exactly do you mucky lot want? Some cleaners are what I am expecting. What are you doing dripping mud all over doorstep?'

'Sorry, sir! My name is Leila', she replied, wringing muddy water from her *jalabiya*. 'I'm here about the cleaning job,' she repeated with an awkward grin.

Before Mr Polonsky could respond, the muddy cyclists, Adam and Sumaya, began to speak, each interrupting the other.

'Um sir, I … I'm here too … er … for the …. job,' Adam said nudging Sumaya.

'No you aren't, I am. I need this job!' she responded angrily, nudging Adam back.

Little Imran peeked out from behind the other three, raising one finger. 'Me too sir,' he said timidly.

The muddy gaggle of kids soon began pulling and shoving each other and bickering.

Mr Polonsky rapped the brass head of his mahogany walking cane against the door frame and raised his right hand, 'As we say in Poland at time like this: SHUT UP!'

Just then a Malaysian-looking boy in jeans and a green shirt, no older than 12, coolly strode up and went straight into the house, humming to himself. Everyone watched him in complete silence. Mr Polonsky shook his head, blinked hard and continued.

'I don't want any noisy, fighting or muddy kids messing up my house. I want cleaner, not dirtier! Are you telling me you are all looking for work here? You all crazy or something? You escape from a home for crazies?' he pointed with his bony finger back towards the street. 'Leave, right now or I call the police! Go on, muddy kids! Leave!'

The kids didn't know what to do.

Just then the Malaysian-looking kid came strolling back out of the house with a bin liner full of rubbish. He stopped at a row of large green wheelie bins and threw it in. Then he turned back to the house and was about to walk back in when Mr Polonsky placed an open palm in front of his face.

'Stop, boy! What you think you are doing?' Mr Polonsky asked, 'you can't just walk in like you own the place!' When no response came he asked the others, 'Do you know this kid?'

They all shook their heads and shrugged their shoulders.

'Humph! Well, young man, who are you? Speak up!' Mr Polonsky asked, raising his voice to a shout.

The kids looked at him waiting for a reply. It was only then everyone realised he was wearing earphones. He pulled out the right earpiece and peered at Mr Polonsky.

'Che Amran's the name,' he said with a smile. 'I'm your new cleaner!' He popped the earpiece back in and began to stroll back into the house.

Mr Polonsky was fuming. 'No no no no, boy! This won't do. Out, or I call the police!'

'But sir,' said Leila, 'I want this job and you haven't even asked me any questions. I want to do a bit of work experience and this is perfect!'

The other kids ummed and ahhed to the same effect; they all wanted the job.

'That's none of my business. All of you leave my house,' said the irate old man, 'You are no good to me. I need real cleaners, not troublemakers - especially ones covered in mud!'

With that Mr Polonsky took one single step backwards and slammed the front door in their faces.

*\*\**

The five kids stood there with their mouths open.

Finally, Adam spoke up, 'well I hate to be the one to say it but – *we been told*!'

Imran shook his head, straightened his baseball cap, and began to shuffle to the front gate. 'Oh well, if he doesn't want our help, let's go, right?' he said looking around to see if anyone else agreed.

Sumaya huffed and scratched her head. 'Hey guys, I just realised whose house this is! They're the Polonskys!'

'Y-you mean *the* Polonskys?' Adam spluttered, 'the couple that tried to hide that burglar from the cops? No way!'

Leila rubbed her chin thoughtfully. 'Ha! I knew the address sounded familiar! "261 North

Row" was all over the papers when it happened. My father said never to go near this house. I assume they've avoided people all this time. No wonder the old geezer made his shop ad anonymous! Crafty!'

'Well, it looks like they need help now,' said Che Amran. 'I have never seen more mess in one place. They must have dozens of pets in there, it looks like a farm in there and like the Hulk got mad and smashed the place up!' he said, puffing out his chest to look like the Hulk. 'By the way,' he continued, 'why is everyone so wet?'

'Long story,' said Sumaya wiping some loose water from her sleeves. 'I would never help people like that, uh-uh! No chance, no way José.'

Imran wagged his head vigorously in agreement.

By now all the kids had left the Polonskys' walkway and were ambling down the road. Adam and Sumaya pushed their bikes alongside them. It seemed they all agreed that none of them would help the Polonskys. They were all set to go their separate ways when Leila suddenly stopped.

'I think we have a duty to help these people,' she started, 'regardless of what they may or may not have done. And think about it, a lot of what was said about them will be rumour and gossip; I mean, come on do you really believe they came from Poland smuggled in Hitler's wardrobe?'

Adam stifled a smirk and spoke up. 'No, haha! I heard that the guy they were hiding turned out to be innocent anyway.' The rest looked confused.

Leila went on. 'We need to think about why we are doing this. I mean, is it just for the money? Or to get work experience? What about you, Adam? Why are you here?'

Adam rubbed his chin and smiled. 'Well, my mum showed me the ad in Violet's shop window. She said it would be extra cash for me. At first I wasn't interested ... until my sister Pam started to tease me.'

'Tease you? About what?' asked Sumaya.

Adam frowned and scratched his head. 'My family is from Jamaica and they are very traditional. Pam doesn't like that I became a Muslim. "You'll soon come back to church" is what she's always saying.'

'You're a convert, or whatever it is?' said Imran.

'Yeah, I've been a Muslim a year now. Anyway, she said that if this religion was good I would help people – like Jesus would!'

'Have you told her Jesus is in Islam too?' said Leila.

'Well, not to her he isn't! She said that if I was still in the Church I would help out, but now that I'm a Muslim ...'

'You won't,' finished Leila.

'Exactly! So here I am. I think we should go back. Well, I'm willing to offer my help. What about you guys?'

Che Amran looked around nervously. Everybody turned to him. Before he spoke he put his hand in his bag and pulled out a pile of papers, 'I just love superheroes. I love the way they jump off the page, it's inspiring ... look!' he held up the bunch of loose papers with pencil drawings on.

The group looked confused.

'I've drawn my own stories and made my own heroes. Each one has a unique power, like this character.' He pointed at a muscular hero with a massively thick neck and broad chin. 'I call him Void from the planet Votta. Would you like to read it?' he asked, shoving the pile of sheets under Adam's nose.

'Ah, ahem ... maybe later!' Sumaya replied.

'Void can teleport anywhere, but when he teleports he destroys the building or thing it's near. That's not all – he can ...'

'Okay, okay! Phew! Just tell us why you're here Che!' said Sumaya rolling her eyes.

'Oh, sorry. I go off on tangents a lot. It's because I have Asperger's syndrome. I'm here just 'cos my mum told me to come.'

'Alrighty then,' exclaimed Adam, turning to Imran. 'What about you? Why are you here?'

'I need some money. I'm saving up to go and see my dad in Holland. He doesn't get to visit us often, so I am planning to stay with him for a week next term break. That's it, really,' said Imran.

It was Leila's turn next. 'Well, like I said to Mr Polonsky, I want some work experience. I'm not worried about the money. Come on guys! Let's go back.'

'Okay!' said Imran nodding his head hesitantly. 'But if we offer to help and he turns us down that's it.'

Sumaya folded her arms and huffed, 'Hmm, OK but I'm telling you now, I have a really bad feeling about this!'

# All hands on deck

S HIMON Polonsky had just settled back into bed. *Cleaners! Some cleaners!* he thought. He had just made up his mind that he might as well sleep for the whole three days until Mrs Polonsky got home, when there was another loud banging at the front door.

'Whaaat?' he roared when he stumbled downstairs and threw open the door. It was the kids. 'You again? Are you going to get lost or do I have to call the police?'

'Look Mr Polonsky we're here to help, okay?' said Leila with a deadpan face. 'We're all together on this. We don't care what people say about you. We can see you really, really need help – don't you?'

Mr Polonsky was struck mute. He had allowed his temper to scare the kids away once and the house was *still* a tip. They could hardly make it worse. After all, how bad could they all be at cleaning anyway? It was rubbish, not rocket science!

'Erm … well …' he glanced at the lobby sideways and winced. 'Okay. I do need some help,' he admitted in a faint voice, his arms flopping to his sides. 'My wife is due back in three days and I've got to do something. She will kill me if the house looks like this.'

'Then that's that. Come on guys, let see what we have to deal with,' said Leila. She was about to step inside when Mr Polonsky stopped her.

'Erm … wait there a minute.' With that he hurried back into the house. The clanking of cutlery could be heard from the kitchen. Then he returned. 'Okay, so now you can start. But I warn you, the mess in here is, well, scarier than a horror film!'

It was true! The house was a complete mess: countless dustbin liners lined the long hallway; the windows were filthy with tattered net curtains; there were chewed newspaper shreds and saw-dust all over the floor; bird droppings littered the handrail of the stairway; all the lights had broken glass fittings; two enormous flower pots had been knocked over; cat litter had been trodden into the thick expensive rugs. And all this was only the hallway of a six-bedroom house!

As the kids entered the house a huge Dalmatian bounded towards Adam, reared on his hind legs and placed its front paws on his chest. Adam, who hated dogs, screamed and bolted upstairs. Three other dogs of assorted kinds excitedly chased him, barking like crazy.

'Adam!' shouted Leila, 'if you run they'll only chase you! Don't run ... don't ... oh goodness me!' she exclaimed swinging her hands in the air and

stamping her right foot. But they were gone. Just then a small black and white kitten snuggled up to Leila's leg.

'Aaaah-choo! Agh, I'm (achoo) allergic to cats, Mr Polonsky,' said Leila. 'Please could you (aaah-choo) take it away?'

Mr Polonsky rolled his eyes. 'Oh come now, it's only Wanda!' But before he could move there was a sudden rumble of hooves as four bearded Billy goats careered down the hallway. Sumaya threw her bag to the floor and dived after one of them – but missed.

'Oi! Come back here!' she said, before turning to the others with a slight blush, 'my auntie in Yemen has a herd of these goats – or something like them anyways. I'll round up these cuties, but get started on the rest of the house, okay? I'll be right back!'

As Sumaya sped off down the hall Che Amran strolled out of the kitchen and tripped over her bag, completely spilling two binliners of rubbish all over the floor.

Mr Polonsky gripped his head and frowned.

'Oh my days, what madness is this? Are you going to break all the possessions too? Why not start with my priceless Ming vase?' As the words left his lips a huge porcelain vase bumped down the stairs and shattered into a thousand pieces at their feet.

'Sorr-yyyy!' shouted Adam as he ran back down the stairs, cradling two longhaired rabbits in his arms while still being chased by the dogs. They were lapping at his heels and had now been joined by four others.

'Leila! Don't just stand there, do something!' he cried hysterically, disappearing around a corner.

'Ach! Your friends are making my place worse! I didn't think that was possible! I have a list of things I need doing, girl! You have to stop them before I have a heart attack!' he exclaimed, mopping his wrinkled face with a handkerchief.

'Shweeeeeeeeeeeeeeeeeeeee!'

A high pitched shrill filled the air from a utility room behind them. It grew louder and louder then changed into a clunking throb, like wet metal crashing together. Mr Polonsky hobbled over and threw open the door. Inside was Imran, frantically turning knobs and dials on a washing machine gone crazy. The machine looked old and battered. It shuddered and bucked. It chugged and glugged. It whizzed and popped! Before anyone could react a jet of water erupted from the washing powder compartment and shot up into the ceiling. It sent a shower of cold water cascading over everyone.

'Aaaahh! I-I can't turn it off! Mr Podonsky, help me! H-how do you turn it off?' screamed Imran.

'It's POL-onsky not POD-onsky, you stupid boy! Why ever did you go and touch Helga! You must never, EVER touch Helga! She is temperamental and she hates it when anyone else but Mrs Polonsky switches her on!'

Leila grabbed Imran by the arm, pulled him away from Helga, the washing machine, and placed him at her back. The frightened boy crouched down behind her covering his head with his arms.

'How do we turn it off?' yelled Leila over the noise of the machine. 'How do we make 'Helga' stop? It looks as though it's about to go into orbit!'

Mr Polonsky tried to protect himself from the shower of falling soapy water while edging toward the machine. He turned several knobs and pushed a few buttons but it bucked and shook even more. The knobs slipped from his grip. A large pool of water covered in soap suds now covered the floor and began to seep out into the hall way!

'Oh no, you've done it now! Only Alexandra can work this contraption. It was her mother's – a family heirloom! Though I've never seen her act so insane before. We have to get out. Come on!' He turned to the door and waved to Leila and Imran to follow, leaving the frantic machine still whirring, chugging and squirting jets of water in every direction. Things didn't look like they could get any worse!

Mr Polonsky, Leila and Imran entered the front hall in shock. They had escaped Helga, but the house was only getting messier. Mr Polonsky was about to say something when Leila put her hand up to his face to silence him. Then she put two fingers into her mouth and blew two loud whistles.

'*Twee-tweet!*'

Everyone – Adam and the dogs chasing him, Che Amran and his bags of rubbish and Sumaya and her galloping Billy goats – stopped dead in their tracks and turned to Leila. She slowly lowered her arms to her sides, turned and looked at each of them.

'Enough! We are *supposed* to be here to help get this house shipshape but so far we have only made it worse!' she said, ankle-deep in soap suds.

Even the dogs chasing Adam whimpered and began to listen. Che Amran peered at her from behind a mound of rubbish and swallowed hard.

'We need to work as a team if we want to get things done around here. Mr Polonsky do you have that list you mentioned earlier?'

He handed her a small note pad with barely legible writing scrawled on it. Leila examined it for a moment, rolling her tongue in her left cheek.

'Hmm, okay everyone, stop what you are doing, (chugga chugga) each of us will (chugga chugga) will ... (chugga chugga) will ... (chug). Oh, that's it! Hold on one minute please,' Leila turned round, entered the utility room and shut the door firmly behind her. The chugging, banging and swirling coming from Helga suddenly stopped. The door opened and Leila calmly walked back into the lobby, smoothing down her clothes and then her hijab.

'Now, as I was saying … doggies?' the ears of the dogs around Adam pricked up.

'Woof?' barked the huge Dalmatian.

'Get back to your own houses, now!'

'Woof, woof?'

'Yes, now!' she ordered, pointing towards the back door.

With tails tucked between their legs, led by the Dalmatian, the pack of dogs sloped off to the door.

'Adam, give those rabbits to Sumaya then grab a mop and bucket and start on the leaking washing machine in the utility room. Imran, help Che Amran to move all these bin liners out. I'll call someone to bring a skip out front where we can throw them all.

The kids set about their tasks like professionals, and that was how it continued.

After a while all the kids began to make real headway in tidying the house. As the day progressed the hallway was clear, the floor polished and the windows cleaned. Leila, who had a great way with electronics, fixed Helga and had her purring like a happy pussycat – which was a great advantage as curtains, bed sheets and clothes had to be washed, ironed and hung in the back garden.

In the garden all the pens and fences used to house the animals were fixed by Adam and Sumaya. Che Amran and Imran threw the rubbish bags in a skip that was parked in the driveway.

On the second day they made a start on the rooms upstairs. It was all done in record time.

On both afternoons at 1.30 and 4.15 the kids stopped whatever they were doing. The first time it happened Mr Polonsky watched curiously as Adam recited something in Arabic before the kids prayed together. He admired the kids' dedication to their prayers and he could see how they all motivated one another. It brought back fond memories of his days helping out his father, who had been the rabbi of the local synagogue in Poland.

\*\*\*

On the day before Mrs Polonsky was due back, the house was sparkling. Mr Polonsky grinned and straightened his shirt collar. He cut a more elegant figure in his clean clothes.

'Well, well, well! I never thought it possible, but you kids have done it. Look at this place!'

Everyone assembled in the large dining room which was now filled with the wholesome smell of wood polish and Shake-n-Vac.

'Oh, Mr Polonsky,' said Leila, 'we have a surprise for you. Sumaya?'

Sumaya placed a length of cloth over the old man's eyes to act as a blindfold.

'Oh what's this?' asked Mr Polonsky, 'am I going somewhere special?'

'Not really,' said Adam, taking him by the arm and leading him into the hallway.

Leila giggled and said, 'You can take off his blindfold now!'

The cloth was quickly pulled away.

'Ta-dah!' said Sumaya, with her arms outspread. 'What do you think?'

Suspended between the banister and a light fitting was a hand-painted banner, six feet long, which read: WELCOME HOME, MRS POLONSKY

Mr Polonsky laughed out loud, clapping his hands together with glee.

'And these flowers are from us too!' said Imran, pointing to a white vase filled with beautiful carnations. Suddenly Mr Polonsky's smile faded.

'Oh how wonderful kids, it makes me so ashamed ... really I'm such an old fool!' he said bowing his head.

'Don't say that, sir,' said Adam patting him on the shoulder.

'No, I am. I-I have something to tell you. You remember when you first came to the house and I ran off back inside for a few moments?' the kids nodded.

'Well, I dashed off to ... to hide our antique silverware. It's been in our family even longer than Helga and is worth a small fortune. I foolishly thought that you would ... rob us! While I was hiding them I dropped a small mustard spoon which fell into Helga's air intake vent. Probably explains why she acted the way she did – hehe.' Mr Polonsky laughed nervously, then gulped.

The kids looked at each other and burst out laughing. Mr Polonsky couldn't help himself and joined in.

'Haha, don't worry about that, Mr Polonsky, I might have thought the same thing if a bunch of muddy kids had knocked on my door!' said Leila.

'Thank you so much. Before you all leave I think we should celebrate with a round of pizzas. Anyone hungry?' he asked rubbing his stomach and licking his lips.

'You're in a room with a bunch of teenagers, Mr Polonsky – of course we're hungry,' laughed Adam.

'As long as it's *halal*, it's cool sir,' added Che Imran, pulling open a small drawer full of takeaway menu leaflets.

'Then it's settled – pizzas all round!' said the old man, reaching for the phone.

# Welcome home, Mrs Polonsky

THE next morning Leila awoke to a strange numbness in her legs. It soon faded and she threw on her clothes, had breakfast and left the house. When she checked her phone she saw that she had three missed calls from Mr Polonsky. She decided to see what he wanted when she got to the house.

Today was Mrs Polonsky's 'release' date and they had all been told to get to the house at 11am sharp. Leila met Imran and Adam outside

Violets shop. Then they walked to the Polonsky's house. As they got close they spied an ambulance parked outside. Two ambulance men speedily walked from the house, jumped in and quickly drove off.

'Hey guys look! Mrs Polonsky must be home early – come on!' said Adam.

As they approached they saw Che Imran and Sumaya standing outside.

'*Salams* guys, is she back?' asked Imran. Che Amran turned to them. He looked very upset.

'*Wa 'alaykum as-Salam*, yeah, she's back but I don't know what's wrong with her!'

'What do you mean?' asked Leila 'What's happened?'

Just then the sound of breaking glass came from the house.

'Does that answer your question?' said Sumaya on the verge of tears. 'I think we just wasted the last three days helping out here! She's gone mad!'

'What do you mean? Tell me what happened,' said Leila.

Sumaya just shook her head disappointedly and added, 'I've had enough. I'm going …

'I'll just go in and ask for myself then!' Leila replied, storming inside.

'Good luck,' shouted Sumaya as Leila disappeared through the door.

'We can't just let her go in,' pleaded Che Amran with the others.

'No! Let her go and find out for herself,' said Sumaya.

The first thing Leila saw was Mr Polonsky sitting on the stairs, staring into space as Wanda, the kitten, sat in his lap trembling. Mr Polonsky tried to calm her by gently stroking her head.

'Mr Polonsky? Are you alright, sir? Is your wife back?' the old man raised his head; there was panic in his eyes.

'I'm sorry my dear Leila, I am so, so sorry.' It was then that Leila saw the welcome home banner had been torn down and ripped to pieces.

'Hey, what's happened here? Have you been burgled? I don't understand what's going on!'

Just then thrashing and banging noises came from the utility room. Someone was in there.

Hearing the clatter, Leila moved to open the door but Mr Polonsky quickly rose to his feet and placed his arm on her shoulder, urging her back outside.

'I want to ... er thank you and your friends for all that you have done. You Muslim kids are all stars but I think ... I think you should ... leave now!'

Suddenly there was a slamming of doors behind them. Wanda sat bolt upright and ran to Leila who instinctively picked her up. The poor thing was trembling more than ever.

'Is that one of those kids you allowed into my house, Shimon?'

It was Mrs Polonsky! She was waving her walking stick in the air.

Mr Polonsky lowered his voice, 'Leila, go now. Please just go.'

But Leila wasn't listening. She ducked under his arm and turned to face Mrs Polonsky.

'There must be some misunderstanding here, Mrs Polonsky. My name is Leila. Your husband asked me and my friends to clean the house ready for your return.'

'GET OUT!' screamed Mrs Polonsky pointing to the front door. 'I don't want you or your friends in my house, manhandling my private property!' she said hobbling towards Leila on her cane. Leila froze on the spot, terrified. Wanda cuddled close.

'But before you go,' added the old woman, 'I take it you have been interfering with Helga. HOW DARE YOU! I should call the police on you just for that. Lucky for you my gullible husband seems to think your 'kindness' is genuine.'

She snatched the bunch of flowers out of the vase.

'Well, here's what I think of your help!' She threw them on the floor.

Leila couldn't believe her eyes. She could feel Mr Polonsky tugging on her right arm.

'Come my dear, when she's like this it's best to leave her alone. Believe me, she'll only get worse.'

'B-but why? What have we done wrong? This is not right,' said Leila, tears swelling in her eyes.

'I know and I'm sorry but please you must leave,' he said with a lump in his throat.

Leila found herself standing outside facing the others. It was only then that she realised that Wanda was still in her arms. The cat didn't make her sneeze at all anymore.

'We heard everything,' huffed Adam. 'I don't know what to say ... I feel like I'm in a bad film.'

In a daze Leila placed Wanda on the door step, rubbed her under the chin and walked away from the house. Not knowing what else to do, the others followed. Only Sumaya remained outside for a moment longer.

'So much for good deeds!' she said before walking in the opposite direction to the others.

Wanda watched as the kids disappeared from view. She placed her head upon her paws and meowed sadly.

Inside the house Mrs Polonsky had to sit down to catch her breath. The anger and fire in her eyes had gone.

'Have they left? Have they finally left, Shimon?' she asked craning her neck to see through the slender glass panels of the front door.

'Yes they have gone, Alexandra. How much longer can you keep this up? You have scared away everyone that's been good to us. It's not fair, it's not right that you should take out your anger on these children. Why must it be like this?'

She stood and hobbled into his arms. She was crying.

'Because they all leave in the end, and what are we left with? N-nothing! Just an empty house, Shimon, filled with memories. Where are our children: Anna, Heidi and Frank? Where are our grandchildren? They're not here because they've abandoned us. They broke our hearts ...'

She gently pulled away and picked up the greeting card fragments and scattered flowers.

' ... and I made a promise that no one will ever hurt us like that again. If they get too close I'll see them off just like Mrs Gates and all the others! Just like I had to do with those children.'

'But this time is different, Alexandra. Do you want these children leaving here thinking all their work was for nothing?'

'They might think that but you still paid them, didn't you? They still got money and that's all kids care about these days!'

'What if I showed you one more good deed they have done for us?'

She stared at him through a curtain of tears.

'What do you mean?' she said drying her eyes.

Shimon pulled a white envelope from his trouser pocket.

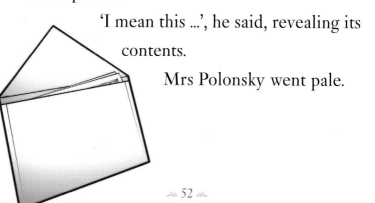

'I mean this ...', he said, revealing its contents.

Mrs Polonsky went pale.

# 'Are we all stars?'

TWO days later Leila, Che Amran, Adam and Imran all sat together in the school canteen. They were still a little shell-shocked after meeting Mrs Polonsky and were all quiet.

'Guys,' said Che Amran scarcely looking up from a drawing he was working on. 'I'm still gutted by what happened but I don't think it should put us off doing, you know, stuff!'

'Stuff?' asked Adam, 'what kind of "stuff" did you have in mind?'

He shrugged his shoulders. 'I don't really know. Why not do something similar?'

'And get shouted at again? No thanks!' said Imran. They all fell silent.

Leila finally cleared her throat. 'He's right! We worked so well together it seems a shame to stop because of one incident!'

'Haha, that wasn't just an "incident", Leila. It was a disaster of epic proportions!' said Adam waving his hands in the air to emphasise his point. 'You know, like the Titanic going down?'

'Well, even so,' she continued 'what did we expect? Did all the people that the Prophet Muhammad – peace be upon him – help, hug him and plaster him with kisses? I admit I was knocked for a loop by what happened but we can't just give up that easily – maybe it's a test?'

A groaning sound left Adams throat.

'If we work together on a regular basis we'll need a team name,' said Che Amran looking up thoughtfully, tapping his pencil against his lips. 'What did Mr Polonsky say? *You Muslim kids are all stars*" We should call ourselves all-stars ... Muslim All-Stars!'

Leila shook her head and rolled her eyes. 'Che, this isn't one of your comics where we have to give ourselves nicknames – I'm not *Hijab Girl* or something silly like that!' she said with a wide grin.

'Who's going to talk to Sumaya? She was really upset and I'm not sure she would want to help,' said Imran.

'Talking about me again, kiddies?' came a voice behind them. It was Sumaya strolling towards them.

'Sumaya! We've not spoken to you since ... well, you know, last time,' said Imran.

Sumaya sat on a bench next to Che Amran who was sketching a superhero, his tongue locked in the corner of his cheek in total concentration.

'Well, I've been thinking. I don't know if I'm interested in helping people again.'

'I don't blame you,' said Adam, 'it was hard to take her turning on us like that, but apparently, it's a test!'

'Ha! A test? You're joking right?' laughed Sumaya shaking her head.

'Everything is a test, Sumaya,' said Leila, raising her eye brows.

Sumaya stood up again and threw her rucksack around her shoulders. Then she turned to the group. 'Yeah, I hear you. And you're right. Tell you what, the next time you guys want to save the world give me a call or text me. If I'm in a good mood I'll see if I can help out.' She gave a mock salute and made for the exit.

'You think she'll join? Join the All-Stars, I mean?' asked Che Amran.

'Che, we are not calling ourselves that,' said Leila rising to her feet. 'But yeah, I think she will.'

'Well, whatever we decide to do,' said Adam, 'we'll have a laugh while we're doing it!'

The bell rang signalling the end of lunch.

The next lesson Sumaya was in class day-dreaming, when the Deputy Head, Mrs Hobbs, came in and approached the teacher, Mr O'Callaghan.

Sumaya laughed to herself, *I bet she's here for Daniel, again. That kid is so bad.* She turned to Daniel's desk, but he wasn't there. *Oh, so who is she here for?*

Mrs Hobbs whispered into Mr O'Callaghan's ear then pointed to Sumaya. Everyone in the class, even the class hamster, Roger, turned to stare at Sumaya.

'Sumaya Abdullahi,' said Mr O'Callaghan, 'go with Mrs Hobbs, please.'

'Why? I ain't done anything!' Sumaya huffed.

'Now, young lady!'

Sumaya rose to her feet, grabbed her bag and followed Mrs Hobbs outside. In the corridor were Leila, Adam, Che Amran and Imran.

'Hey, you lot! What's going on? Where are we going?' asked Sumaya.

Leila leaned into her and whispered. 'We're going to the Headteacher's office, not sure why though. My mum will freak when she hears I've gotten into trouble – simply freak.'

Adam looked over to them.

'My friend Lauren Booth said that someone's complained about us. Someone local! I think you can guess who,' he said, raising his eyebrows.

Leila coughed. 'You mean Mrs Polonsky? Yeah, I bet you're right.'

'Will we get expelled?' asked Imran who was wide-eyed and scared. 'Oh God, mum will go ballistic.'

'Listen guys, I've been in trouble loads of times. Just keep cool and let me do all the talking,' said Sumaya with a wink.

In the office was the Headteacher, Mrs Battyhaliks, Leila's mother, Mr Polonsky and sitting quietly, with a face like sour milk, was Mrs Polonsky. As the kids entered Mr Polonsky gave a weak smile. It was spotted by his wife who gave him a cutting look of disapproval.

'Mum,' started Leila, but her mother indicated for her to remain quiet by placing her index finger to her lips. 'Just wait a moment, Leila. The Headteacher has a few things to say.'

'Now then,' said Mrs Battyhaliks taking a seat, 'unfortunately at such short notice I was only able to get hold of Leila's mother. As for the rest of you, your parents have been notified and I will phone them later. Mrs Polonsky here says she has a serious complaint to discuss with us. So, for now, I want you all to remain silent and hear what Mrs Polonsky has to say.'

The Head Teacher turned to Mrs Polonsky. 'Now, Mrs Polonsky, you told us you had a serious complaint regarding these students. Perhaps you would like to tell us what they have done?'

Mrs Polonsky sat back in her chair, her hands gripping the head of her cane. 'I have a complaint all right. I am disgusted and appalled that in this day and age these kids can come into my house ...'

Adam shook his head and stood up, 'No! Mr Polonsky told us we could come in to help clean the house ...'

'Young man, you'll be given a chance to respond in a short while!' said the Headteacher, waving him back to his seat. Adam slumped back into his chair with a scowl.

Mrs Polonsky cleared her throat. 'Ahem! As I was saying ... while I was away in hospital they came into my house and tampered with my things ...'

'No, no!' shouted Sumaya. 'We didn't do anything wrong! We all had letters from our parents saying it was okay!'

All the kids nodded their heads. The headteacher held her hands up for silence.

'I understand that but I want you to hear Mrs Polonsky out. You may be surprised by what she has to say!'

The kids looked at each other curiously.

'I understand you are all upset, so am I,' continued the old woman. 'I am upset that you children came into my house for three days and fixed the fences, cleared up all the rubbish and fed the animals.' A single tear began to roll down her cheek. 'You treated my husband with kindness and respect even after he shouted at you. I thank you from the very bottom of my heart.' She pulled out a tissue and blew her nose.

There was total silence in the office. Leila, Mrs Hobbs and even Imran had tears in their eyes. Sumaya was choked up but refused, as always, to show it.

'Ahem, th-that's what this is all about?' Sumaya said. 'You're here to thank us?' She glanced over to Mr Polonsky, who was smiling and wiping his eyes with a handkerchief. He knelt down and hugged Mrs Polonsky. 'You did it, Alexandra. You did it. I am so proud of you. The children would be proud of you too.'

'But I'm not finished.' She cleared her throat and stood up. 'My complaint is that such wonderful kids are in our community and the school tells no one. This is outrageous!' She jabbed the point of her cane into the floor. 'Such deeds should be shouted from the rooftops – or reported in the local paper at the very least!' she continued, wagging her finger. 'I am ashamed to say that when

I saw what they had done for our home and saw the welcome sign, I acted ... like a fool. My husband and I have had some terrible experiences with our own kids. In Yiddish we call it a '*Shtuken Nisht in Harts*', which means a stab in the heart. But I had no right to take it out on any of you. Please, please forgive me.' She began to tremble.

The kids all looked at each other. 'Y-y-y-yeah er ... I mean yeah, we accept,' stuttered Imran, looking at Leila.

'Of course we do, Mrs Polonsky,' said Leila, gently placing her hand on the woman's shoulder.

'But you were so mad at us! What made you change your mind?' asked Che Amran.

She smiled and reached into a straw bag at her feet and pulled out the white envelope.

'What is that?' asked Leila's mother.

'This,' replied Mrs Polonsky, pulling out a bundle of cash, 'is the money that was supposed to pay the children for their work in the house. But they told my Shimon to give it to charity instead.' Again tears formed in her eyes. 'They have overwhelmed me with their kindness, bless them.'

Leila's mother nodded and gave her daughter an approving smile, her bottom lip quivering.

The Headteacher rose to her feet, waving her hands. 'Mr and Mrs Polonsky, I can assure you that everything these students have done will be reported to the Tribune newspaper. I'll see to it myself. And of course we have the school bulletin too! But for now I think a hearty round of applause is in order, don't you?'

Mrs Polonsky nodded as she joined the other adults in their applause. She leaned over to Leila. 'Just one more thing, my dear.'

'Yes Mrs Polonsky, anything!'

'How on earth did you get Helga to behave?'

Leila smiled and whispered something into the woman's ear. After a moment or two Mrs Polonsky burst out laughing and said, 'If I could bottle that I'd be a millionaire, sweetheart! And call me Alexandra.' Then she raised her hands

to gain everyone's attention. 'I am told by my husband that you all love pizza. Well, it would be my pleasure to invite you all round to my nice clean home for *halal* pizza after school today! How about it guys?'

A cheer of 'Yay, that's cool!' went up from the kids.

After being dismissed by the headteacher they all made for the door.

'So what is next for you all?' asked Mr Polonsky. Che Amran turned to him and said, 'Hmm not sure really but as long as it isn't cleaning up after animals we'll be happy.'

# Glossary

**Asperger's syndrome** a rare and relatively mild form of autism. Sufferers have very narrow interests and find it awkward to communicate with others.

**As-salamu 'alaykum / Wa 'alaykum as-salam** May peace and blessings be upon you / and upon you be peace. (*Salams* is a commonly used shorthand).

**Hijab** head scarf worn in public by Muslim women.

**Halal** meat prepared according to Muslim law.

**Jalabiya** a long gown.

**Yiddish** one of the three major languages of Jewish history.

# Aknowledgements

I would like to thank Almighty Allah for continuing
to bless me in all my efforts and making them bear fruit.

I would also like to thank Hakim, Shakira and Daniella for
their continued support and understanding in all that I do.